THE SONS OF
MACOMISH

STORIES BY
TOM BRYAN

illustrated by Peter Hay

For Sitar

Warm regards

T By

TWO RIVERS PRESS
READING

In Memoriam
Iain Crichton Smith
(1928–1998)
who encouraged so many of us in the North

Is fheàrr na 'n t-òr sgeul
innse air choir
Better than gold is a tale rightly told
Gaelic proverb

Acknowledgements:
Andy Mitchell, Herr K. Mattner,
Donald S. Murray, Archie MacDougall (1927–1999),
Anne MacLeod, Janet Paisley and to the Highland
people whose generosity and kindness will
never be forgotten.

Published in Great Britain 2000 by
Two Rivers Press
35-39 London St
Reading RG1 4PS

text © Tom Bryan
illustrations © Peter Hay

designed by Matthew Holtby

ISBN 1 901677 27 3

Contents

Famine Road
(*Potato Death Recipes*)

Recipe One: A Recipe for Disaster
Edsel Blues – potatoes with skins of smooth marble, maincrop, going in this April day.

There are many voices planting today:

A good day for it.
Aye.

Grand day for it.
Aye, aye.

Fine day for it, man.
Fuckin' fine, aye.

Previous week, not much rain, soil now moist but not water-logged. Sun squinting through the ash tree, always the last to leaf.

The ground is rough, full of tree roots, well-shaded. Bottles come up, rusted barbed wire, old pennies with corroded Royal faces tinged with green. Spade slices fat white grub worms. The rake peels back matted grass, dry like dead skin, exposing the clay-streaked soil underneath.

Soor ground.
Richt soor. Don't expect much, mind.
Roots and stones. Tardy ash, gale-blasted hemlock, striven

butterfly bush; this all crossed and fertilised by deer, hedgehogs, badgers, errant sheep, foxes and pine martens. I build a cairn of fist-sized stones taken from the ground.

Edsel Blues. Sounds like a song. 'Since my baby left me...' She has left, but not for good. My wife Shona. I took her to the bus yesterday to visit her god-daughter Linda who is ill in hospital. Linda is dying of anorexia. She is fifteen but weighs six stone and is being kept alive by force feeding through tubes. Linda went into a coma yesterday. Shona said: 'I will... I will stay on for the funeral.'

I've never met Linda but I did see a photograph once. A teenager with curly brown hair and deep eyes. She was in a spangly lavender dancing costume. She looked like a strong awkward calf. She was grinning; in fact, her whole young body was grinning.

Edsel Blues but the earth I dig is black; cold and black.

Recipe Two: The Growing

I'll need to put in a few rows of first earlies: Javelins, maybe, or Duke of Yorks. They grow as though in a silly, speeded up film. Quick unfolding leaves, the surprising hardness of the first shoots, short-lived flowers, and the haulms of many colours. By the first week of July I will gather mottled potatoes looking like chicken eggs and boil them in fresh mint leaves until the skins peel and split; salt and butter will go into the wounds. I will eat them along with small trout from the Avainn Mor, toasted in oatmeal; a splooter of real cream would be just right.

Pulling potatoes from rough ground the fingernails fill with hard earth causing them to bleed onto the thin-skinned potatoes. Blood and potatoes.

Recipe Three: The Enemies of Potatoes

Phtophtora infestans: a fungus which ate potatoes, so that people couldn't; this tiny living thing killed millions of people because it liked to eat potatoes. Roots, haulms, leaves: wireworm, blight, fungus, slugs, rabbits, and unseen legions, invisible and deep, the white flesh bored, plumbed and blackened.

Coming to Britain many years ago, I marvelled at the posters and leaflets warning against Britain's most unwanted immigrant, the Colorado Potato Beetle. Emigration full circle. I could imagine the signs on boarding houses and jobsites:

DOGS, IRISH AND POTATO BEETLES NOT
WELCOME; IRISH AND POTATO BEETLES
NEED NOT APPLY

The Colorado Potato Beetle was an old friend of mine. I knew him well.

As a boy, shirtless in sticky Canadian summers, I gathered Potato Beetles in a jam jar, their black and yellow (like tiny football strips) shellacked by the morning dew. I filled the jar and took them proudly to my grandfather who took the jar and smiled at me, giving me each time a shiny new Canadian dime. His father had left Ireland at the height of the potato Famine, leaving his own parents dead of typhus in a ditch in East Limerick. My grandfather held the jar aloft to the light. I never knew what he did with the beetles but the jar always came back empty.

Recipe Four: Desert Island Potatoes
Trapped on a desert island, you are allowed one vegetable for survival.

I would choose the common potato: *Solanum tuberosum.* Vitamins A, B, C, protein, carbohydrate, calcium, iron, phosphorus, potassium; first aid – relief of burns, ideal poultice. Potato wine, whisky, beer, soup, pie, cakes, chutney, chowder, dumplings, bread, salad. Chantilly, Charlotte, O'Brien. Canapes, nests, patties, souffle, stuffed, scones, stovies, clapshot, mashed, scalloped, sauteed, baked, boiled, broiled, fried, colcannon. *Buntata:* Irish, the love of my heart, you lovely potato, you alone fed five million people for two hundred years in lazy beds in plots only the size of a rich man's swimming pool.

Shona is on the phone. 'Linda is coming out of the coma. Matchstick thin, eyes sinking into her head... they couldn't force feed her any longer. But she'll make it.'

I would send Linda (from my dreams) a wonderful cake of Kerr's pink potato swirled with cream and the lightest of spices, rich in all the good things thriving in limestone soil. I would spoon it to her like a baby, until those eyes shone once more like wet chestnuts. Shona said her god-daughter could soon be spoon-fed.

Death and Potatoes, but Life and Potatoes too. Always a fine balance.

Recipe Five: Black Rain on the Famine Road
Shona's family goes a long way back here. Camerons. They helped build the Destitution Road. The Famine Road, dug by starving men to earn money for food. Works relief. Some of those Camerons survived or Shona would not be here. 'This is a Winter of Starvation,' said a Skye minister in 1846, a year when three quarters of the population of the North West Highlands was entirely without food.

My own story from Ireland is the story of millions. My great grandfather would not grow potatoes in Canada. He preferred maize so he could see everything above ground, in the clear light of day. 'Death doesn't like sunlight,' he once said.

Shona back on the phone. 'Linda is fine, she is grinning again…
but did you hear about the explosion at Chernobyl? If you
haven't you are the only one in the world who hasn't.'

I have heard, now. Gases and poisons from across the great
wheat fields of Silesia, potato-shaped clouds blowing west, full
of diseased rain, coming this way. Blowing West, 'Gone West';
gone west, –fur trapper slang for dying; the old Irish used the
same expression.

Recipe Six:
During the day, the cloud is above my window, the same way
Orion is at night. My potato haulms are hard and green, straight
and true, leaves waxen and eager. First earlies, the earthing up
ritual going on today in this Strath, westwards to the Islands, to
the great marram grasses, to the deep lush turf of Caithness
and Sutherland; and now we are earthing up under a dark cloud
– a dark cloud ready to piss and shit its kack down onto our
leaves and haulms, soaking deep into the tubers, sizzling
valuable microbes and bacteria, bleaching and frying the under-
ground nutrients.

The rain has stopped but a cloud still blots the sun.

Shona says Linda's eyes are sparkling now, dark and vibrant.

The Featherless Biped
meets the Giant Squid

The old man lived in a 'bender' made of white birch saplings covered by a tattered green tarpaulin. Smoke circled from a crooked chimney made of a biscuit tin. The site was a clearing near the local tip, surrounded by spindly gorse, fencing wire and discarded oil drums. The man was dressed for the cold even though it was the height of summer. He scuttled around, in heavy vests, woollen jumpers and layers of greasy yellow oilskins reaching down to the tops of his faded black wellies. He was not tall. Two dark eyes peered out of a weathered face, covered in a mat of nicotine-stained beard. He boiled water on a small calor gas stove, propped up on a discarded school desk.

John Campbell, a twenty year old Canadian, rode his bicycle daily past the site. He'd come to Scotland to visit relatives. His father had been disturbed at a restlessness in his son and was hoping this Scottish 'adventure' would cure the boy of a current notion of dropping his accountancy studies in order to travel around the world. The father hoped his son would eventually join the firm as an accountant. Meanwhile, young Campbell was mending wooden fish boxes on the pier while staying alone in a caravan at his aunt's house five miles up the road. He had to cycle this single-track road to work: there was no other road.

Daily, the old man scuttled around the site and added to his pile of camp furnishings. The junk piled up so high that only the smoke curling up from the tent was visible from the road. He saw the gangly dark-haired youth cycle past twice each day, noting how the boy increased the push bike speed when he drew even with the site. The boy is feart, thought the old man, opening a tin of cold beans and scooping the sauce from the lid with a yellow finger. He poked the finger through the bushy beard. Some beans remained stuck in the bristles. One day, the old man crossed the road to the burn to get fresh water for the kettle. He stepped out from behind a huge rock just as Campbell swerved to miss him. The bike ended up in a ditch.

'You all right son? Good, I'm Hamish by the way, who the hell are you?'

The boy dusted his jeans off. There was a rip just below the knee. 'I'm... I'm... John Campbell from Canada. I'm working in the village... staying at my aunt's down the road... I... I... didn't mean to frighten you.'

'It's not me that's frightened son, have a cup of tea?'

He saw the boy hesitate.

'I'm not dangerous boy. *Au contraire*. What's the crack by the way?'

The boy drew back, puzzled.

'Crack, son. You know, gossip, news. What brings you to these sunny shores?'

The boy told him about Toronto and accountancy and the mending of wooden fish boxes. 'But what I'd really love to do is travel. I'd like to go to Asia and Australia.'

Hamish snorted and continued shovelling baked beans into his mouth with a fork. The thick sauce stuck to his moustache. He wiped it off with a finger which he then stuck into his mouth. He crushed the can then tossed it into a gorse bush.

'Not much of a place Australia. No culture. No philosophy. Too much sunshine. Not good for a person, too much sunshine.'

The boy stood up. 'Thanks for the tea.'

The old man grunted.

'See you again,' he said as he cycled off with a wave.

Not bluidy likely, thought Hamish.

Campbell cycled up the road, his mind returning to the old man and the cluttered site. My mind is cluttered just like that, he thought. He cycled down the single-track road, past forests of birches and stands of gorse. Thinking of his father's air conditioned office in Toronto, John Campbell gripped his bike so tight his knuckles turned white.

He saw the old man again the next day. Hamish was sitting on an upended Walls Ice Cream box, eating beans out of a tin with a pocket knife. He offered the boy the ice cream box, then sat down on a pile of oilskins on the ground. Hamish farted loudly. 'A kiss for you son,' he laughed. 'So John Campbell, when I was a youth in Lochaber many years ago, I first heard of Plato. Plato once defined man as simply "a featherless biped". Someone chucked a plucked chicken at the great philosopher and said here's a "man" then. I later went into a Seminary and thought about what a featherless biped I had been. Accountancy or Australia? A helluva choice if you ask me. The choice between cat shit and dog shit. If they say accountancy, I would advise Australia. I've been to the Antipodes with the Merchant Navy. I get a pension... buy what I need and travel on. As the Yanks say, three hots and a cot. Three hot meals and a place to sleep. Mainly, I try to stay warm and dry. I've got my places picked out you see... my wee itinerary. From Cape Wrath to Whithorn. I never go to England.'

John Campbell poked the ground with a stick, making swirling lines which tapered off into the dust. 'I'm not ready to settle in one place. I'd like to travel while I'm young and healthy. I think there's more to life than what you see on the surface...'

Hamish raised an eyebrow at the last word. He drew circles in the dirt with his wellie boot.

'There is more to life than what's on the surface but life is too short to waste it on travel.'

The old man went silent and waved the boy away.

The next day, Campbell cycled past and saw the old man was gone, even though the site was still cluttered.

The boy missed him somehow, even though he feared the old man in some way. His aunt had cautioned him to leave the old man alone. 'A daft old bugger. Steer well clear of him, John.' A week later, on the way home, the boy saw the rising smoke from the bender. The old man was back. John went over to the fire and the old man came out of the tent. 'Just in time for a cup of tea son. Pull up a chair. Just picked up my pension.'

Campbell noticed Hamish had scrubbed his face. His oilskins looked new.

'I've a few vices right enough. Tobacco and a snort of whisky now and then, for medicinal purposes. Use it sparingly.' He proffered a hip flask which the boy refused.

'Ah, I thought so, son. Never mind, boy, you'll catch your germs from somebody else. Leave the girls alone. They unsettle your mind. Want to hear a theory of mine? No answer? Listen. All life centres around one event: an *Erklarung*, Illumination, *satori*, revelation. Things happen and we change, forever. Maybe that's why old men like me live in benders and travel up and down the land. Remember in the Bible, the devil was condemned to walk up and down in the world. Poor bugger, forever walking up and down in the world.'

The midges rose up around the boy's head. They didn't seem to bother the old man. I will see this through, he thought. The old man is drunk. Hamish interrupted the awkward silence. 'Son, I'm knackered.' He farted, then belched. 'Too much drink. I'll tell you my story tomorrow. Illumination. The big event that changes a man's – or a boy's – life.' He staggered to the tent. John heard a series of farts from the tent. Soon, he heard the old man snoring. The boy sat at the fire and watched the stars come out and then got on his bike and cycled home. It was still light enough to see the road. The boy arrived at his caravan, lit the gas light and made a cup of tea. He thought about the old tramp. He found the old man irritating – sometimes boring and rude, but he contrasted Hamish's way of speaking with his father's. Young Campbell grinned at the thought and took another sip of tea. He would hear this thing out. He would hear what the tramp had to say.

The next day was wet and windy, cold for the summer. Cycling home, Campbell saw the old man's fire blazing up. He went over to the fire and sat down on the ice cream box. Hamish emerged from the tent. He belched and stretched. He scuttled over to the fire and put a kettle on the grate propped up on two rocks either side of the fire. He took a hip flask from his oilskin pocket, swigged it back, wiped his mouth with his greasy sleeve, and began: 'I was in the Merchant Navy years ago – a "sparks" – radio operator. This was before I went into the Seminary. I've been everywhere: America, Canada, Mao's China, Russia, Australia. Everywhere. Seen it all. Fights, riots, women, drugs. Also, a helluva lot of boredom. The ocean can be boring…'

Campbell raised an eyebrow. Hamish continued.

'There is a lot of boredom on the sea. Not under the sea though. What's under the surface, that's what life's about. Don't laugh. Are you listening?'

'Yeah, yeah,' said Campbell. The midges had come down. Hurry up, he thought, for Chrissakes hurry up.

Hamish belched and continued.

'We were off the coast of Western Africa – Angola – on a lovely day in the summer, many years ago. Clear sky, clear sea, smooth surface. One of the men said he saw something off port side.'

Hamish took another swig and spat into the fire. The spit hissed. Campbell rubbed his eyes with his jacket sleeve, eyes raw from midge bites. 'A lot of us were on deck and saw something on the surface of the sea. We took the ship in closer and saw a huge Moby floating on the water. Moby, you know, what we called the big sperm whales, like Moby Dick in the story. This lovely grey creature was just floating on the calm surface. Usually, a Moby will dive when a ship gets near but this one didn't. He just lolled in a seasick kind of way. Then we saw the blood. He was bleeding from the blowhole and corners of his mouth. He was badly injured, maybe from a ship's propeller. We couldn't go in any closer because of the rocks along the coast.'

Campbell could see agitation in the old man's features even though the midges weren't going near him. Hamish poked at the fire. He wrapped his oilskin cuff around his fingers and shifted the hot kettle to another part of the grate.

'Fancy some tea, son?'

'No, no that's OK.'

Hamish poured the water into a pewter mug with no handles. He left the tea bag in the mug and took a slurp of the boiling tea. Some of it dribbled in small rivulets through the yellow beard. The rain had stopped and the midges were coming down in droves. Campbell stood up.

'No, sit down son, we're no finished yet. Then, this big Moby, over sixty feet long, went under the water in a swirl of blood. He turned once and was gone. Then, none of us will ever forget what we saw next. We saw huge tentacles rise up out of the water and we saw the shape of a gigantic squid boiling just beneath the surface. It lifted the whale in the air once more and slowly pulled it down. The huge whale went down like a child's toy. The ship had to turn away but we watched with binoculars. The ocean was soon calm. Like nothing had ever happened.'

Hamish stood up and kicked the ashes of the fire.

'Just two large animals fighting in the sea. It must happen all the time, eh, smart arse? That's it, that's my life story. My illumination.'

Campbell stood up, puzzled at the old tramp's belligerence. Hamish had disappeared into the tent. The boy could hear him belching and coughing.

John Campbell cycled down the road in the drizzle. He passed the familiar birches which looked thin and ghost-like in the dusk. A few stars were trying to shine through the thin gauze of mist and rain. A light breeze had come in from the sea, dispersing the midges. Campbell stopped at the top of the hill and leaned his bike against a skinny rowan tree. He sat down on a wet rock and looked out to the sea, now mottled and dappled by the soft rain. The image of the whale and the giant squid kept appearing in his mind. He kept puzzling over the purpose of the story and the old man's agitation at telling it. He watched the sea until it was too dark to see anything. The rain had begun to pelt down. He walked slowly down to the sea and reached into his pocket. It was a return air ticket, Glasgow to Toronto. He took a deep breath and tore the ticket into many pieces, which he threw onto the rain-pocked sea. The tiny white pieces floated briefly, then sank slowly, one by one.

Inhaling the Truth

Tadeuz who lives up the street sometimes comes in for the crack and a dram, or a cup of tea. He is a grinning man who gardens and repairs bicycles. His face is the colour of a new strawberry. His hair is grey. (He says his hair has always been grey.) He is Polish but his accent is pure Inverness and his manner is mostly Highland. He also rolls cigarettes like an artist – cleanly, deftly, coolly – without wasted motion.

He pulls his chair closer to mine, puffing small rings into the air, thoroughly enjoying every puff.

'It is like this,' he begins, as the smoke rings form tiny quivering halos above his head.

'Ah, Poland.'

He inhales deeply and releases the smoke with a sigh.

'Hitler came in an squeezed the left one… he squeezed our manhood. Then Stalin came in an squeezed the right one until we coughed up our dignity. I had just turned sixteen and had not yet slept with a woman. Imagine, going to war to die before making love.'

The smoke rings disintegrate like ripples on a quiet pond.

'They took the young men of our town who had no guns and marched us to the local school. The Germans kept us there until the Russians came. The Russians took us in a hay cart to a camp on the border. I knew the place well. I had often picked mushrooms there as a boy. We came from everywhere: Ukrainians, Poles, Germans, Gypsies, Czechs – from everywhere. We slept in long bunkhouses. Hell, you know the type.

Like in the old war films. We had no real work to do and the Russians just wanted us to keep out their hair. I spent all my time thinking about girls, talking and smoking. Good crack. I also read one helluva lot.'

I was puzzled at this: 'Reading and smoking? Hell, Tadeuz, where did you manage to get cigarettes and books in such a place?'

Tadeuz laughs. 'It was this way. The Russian guards were keen on *Pravda* which of course means "Truth" in Russian. Our guard was a young Tartar whose mother was Polish. He pretended to hate us Poles. At first, he just walked past with a sneer and said: "Put your faith in your bayonet and put your bayonet in the Polack." But we often talked in Polish just to pass the time of day. Gradually, I learned enough Russian to impress the guard and I eagerly asked him for his old copies of *Pravda*. He was pleased to do it, thinking he had converted me to the Red Cause of Mother Russia.'

Tadeuz is now shaking with laughter and the cigarette smoke bounces off his ruddy cheeks.

'Aye, aye – *Pravda, The Truth.* Man I couldn't lose. I was in good with the guards who considered me a real 'Tovarisch-Comrade' but I kept in with my fellow prisoners as well.'

I ask him how that could be. Wouldn't being in good with the guards cause suspicion among his fellow prisoners?

'No, man, I was winning on all fronts, unlike the bloody Germans. I was learning Russian, thus getting free copies of *Pravda* – toilet paper, man, toilet paper. Better than grass, sticks or leaves. And very good insulation for our boots. No man in that camp ever lost toes to gangrene or frostbite. Best of all, it made lovely cigarette papers. Perfect. Our feet were warm, our arses were clean and we never ever ran out of smokes. All this helped me stay alive, you see, to save myself for a good girl after the War.'

Tadeuz' meaty hands are rolling another cigarette on my kitchen table. He is a true artist and survivor. His eyes twinkle as he sucks in the smoke with a great laughing gulp. His laughter echoes throughout the kitchen. His smoke rings dance crazily above his head. He rises to go, saying:

'A man could do far worse, you know, than to inhale the Truth.'

Sandman

They call me Sandeman the Sandman. I am what they call me: a self-employed carter of sand: for cement, mortar, road-building, garden filler. My sand is of excellent quality. I know sand.

My real name had nothing to do with sand or its uses. When the long ships came to their Southern land, the Norsemen had with them *Sandemaend*, the 'men of truth.' In those old Norse countries, the Sandemaen were men of integrity who were required to give witness in court in cases of assault, murder and theft. Their word was as good as evidence and sent many guilty men to their deaths. Likewise, their intervention acquitted many men and gave them life. The men of truth.

Mr Sandeman: an overweight bachelor who lives alone with a three year old collie bitch named Sandie. I own a new bungalow and a blue flatbed truck, a Bedford, whose bed has been polished for years by grains of silicon. It is my delivery truck. I am local so there is some gentle fun with me and my name. I've heard it all before:

Mr. Sandman, make me a dream.

What's for dessert? Sand.

And from children: is it true, your favourite food is a *sand*wich? Heh, heh.

But it is friendly. Sure, they take the piss about my love of sand. My Headmaster said:

'Sandeman, if you could study sand you would be a world authority, a Distinguished Professor of Sand. Alas, Sandeman, there is more to life than sand. There is Mathematics, English and Chemistry, to name but a few. Leave this school knowing you could have been a Master of Silica. Good luck Sandeman.'

I had very little luck, but when my old folks died over ten years ago, they left me enough money to build a new bungalow and buy a new delivery truck.

When I get home from work, I feed Sandie, have my own tea, then set out my 'work' on the kitchen table. I'll explain my work, my book. There are two parts to it. One is sand in general, the other I might call the darker side of The Sandman, of the 'other' work I do. Remember, the old Sandemaen could give life or take it. Remember that.

I'm making notes:

Chapter One: The Quest

Sand is a hard granular powder, mostly impure silica. Around here it is quartz, but pure quartz sand is rare and unknown to me. I still seek that pure quartz. My source of sand is private, secret to me. Of sand, my favourite sandy places:

Achmelvich: the sand here is even whiter when the sea is greenest.

Achnahaird: wider than the sea itself, not so white as Achmelvich but has other good properties.

Luskentyre: don't call this a beach, call it a desert. This is heaven to any man of sand.

Coral (lime) sand: This is found across the great tropical seas. I would like to see this one day if I ever go on holiday.

Gypsum sand: this is said to be pure snowy white.

Composition: I can tell the composition of sand by just running it through my fingers. Magnetite, monazite, garnet, ilmenta, rutile. My life will be too short to run every type of sand through my fingers.

Sand is the soft brown sugar of any recipe. It stirs in, mixes, disappears, yet determines the final outcome – is the final outcome of any use it is put to. This study of sand will include:

The Geology of Sand
The History of Sand
Current Uses of Sand
Sands of the World
Sands of Scotland

I've spoken to a few people about my book. It is a source of some local amusement but people are kind.

– The book, oh aye, how goes that book by the way?

– Oh no, here comes Sandeman, for Christ sake don't get him on the subject of sand.

– I bet he has newspapers with only sand on Page Three.

And so on. There is what I call the darker side of Sand and I'm not sure how this is related to the rest of my book - to the Uses of Sand, for example. Remember how in the Bible the devil is always 'walking up and down in the world'. I drive up and down in the world and have delivered sand to nearly every house and business in a thirty mile radius. I wonder always, what can a sandman do? The songs tell us. Children wake up with sealed eyes, softly glued shut, gritted for sleep and dreams. So the sandman had a twofold task:

1) To close the eyes, producing sleep.

2) To bring dreams and the peace that comes from dreaming.
Mr. Sandman, bring me a dream.

I don't seem able then, to be a good sandman. This leads to Part Two: *Pure Quartz Sand, or The Dark Side of Sand.*

I drive out with 14 bags of hundredweight of good dry silicon base. I put the tarp over the load, to ensure its dryness. I drove down to the river to the cottage called Gillaroo (the Red Boy) to get the key to the big house where I will be delivering the sand. The door was open. I called 'James' three times, then went in. He was there in the living room, twitching on the end of a rope tied to the eaves. I took his weight over my left shoulder and cut him down with my right hand, with a knife I always carry. I laid him down on a carpet with red dragons on it. He never opened his eyes. And that was the first time the Sandman brought sleep but not dreams. That would not be the last time.

You see, I drive all over this hard country, to houses grimed with hurt and pain and I deliver sand and get secrets in return. Where I live people do not end life with posh pills and only a few own guns, but good rope is available to all.

The next time was a year later. An old man was still kicking on the rope when I cut him down too, then he just coughed and died. Again, no dreams from this Sandman, just sleep.

Those days of rain and the dark kach that kicks the life out of the hillside, driving smoke back down chimneys under a moon that is rising even before the bairns come home from school, and I know from the smokeless chimneys that there will be a jumper there, a 'leaper' who is leaping into dreams or escaping nightmares and I the Sandman will cut him down, closing his eyes.

But there are some survivors on the sand run too. They are mostly older women who will never leap or fly but instead prison themselves 'against the market place'. These fear to go outdoors. They keep this secret from their husbands, doctors, children and social workers. They cook, iron, clean and sew. They ask me, the sandman, about the sun, sky and stars; about the local gossip. I am a lifeline to their wider world. My visits are just like visits to a prisoner who has been jailed for life.

And what dreams from the Sandman who has time for a cup of tea and a pleasant human word from 'the outside'. That is the sand I deliver – dreams and hope – maybe for those ones who

will never leap. But I know more will leap and I will cut them free and close their eyes. Maybe those leapers will find the pure quartz I seek in vain.

The Woodcarver's Tale

We all felt it – something in the air those first years into the next Millennium. We were young enough to look mainly to the future. We knew our tales would be told; our songs would be sung. However, it took an old man to remind us that nothing is new, that the past will always be with us and that Highland life is always built on the bedrock of that past. He reminded us what responsibility was – what it would always be…

Mind you, the woodcarver took responsibility further than most of us – he thought he was responsible for the deaths of thirty million people…

I worked for the estate that autumn with him and two others, gathering brood fish for a re-stocking programme. The two 'boy racers' in one boat, the woodcarver and myself in the other. 'He's a daft bugger, but shouldn't be in Craig Dunain. Harmless, aye, harmless,' they whispered to me, while rowing out to Hazel Island.

The woodcarver had a name, Roderick. Thin and gnarled like the oak wood he carved. He carved while I rowed. The old boat took in water which he bailed with a coffee tin. We set the long fyke nets, once used for eels, marking them with the buoy. Each morning we would lift one net and empty the brood trout into plastic buckets. We threw the smaller ones back. Buckets full, we rowed ashore where a lorry with oxygenated tanks took the fish up to the estate for sorting into ripe males and females.

We took breaks and lunch in the old tin-roofed sheep pen next to the cemetery. The drystane dyke surrounding the cemetery was crumbling in places and the Scots pine in the centre of the graveyard was bent to the ground by years of wind. Most of the gravestones had fallen over and the writing on all of them was barely legible. Lichen filled in the letter grooves, giving an impression of all the names and dates being written in green-blue ink.

The shore dipped steeply to the loch which was studded with small islands covered in native trees and rare flowers, since sheep and deer could never graze there. Three mountains bearded the loch:

A serrated shark's tooth
A woman's cleavage, with blouse-like snow
A ski ramp

The boy racers (both Mackenzies but unrelated) kept mainly to themselves, rolling spliffs, sharing their own private jokes. Woodcarver smoked a pipe, drawing his sharp carving knife down the wood, shavings piling up like potato peels at his feet. After lunch, we'd take another fyke net and return the full one. It was a race against the winter gales.

An early November day, grass hard in frost, cold mist rising from the loch, now churning grey in the wind. We couldn't go out until the weather settled or blew over. The boy racers were bored.

'Hey, carver, have one of these. Cheer you up.' A racer proffered a joint to the old man (they knew I didn't smoke). The old man never looked up. The other boy racer chimed in: 'Tell new boy here about how you should have saved thirty million people...'

The carver pulled the knife, finishing the stroke. He folded the knife, put the long piece of carved oak into a bale of straw. He walked out into the rain. 'Daft old cunt,' they laughed

30

in unison.

I rowed and lifted nets for a month. The carver, while pleasant, spoke to me only a few times. 'Grand day,' or 'Son, I don't trust that knot,' and I'd then have to form the knot again until he was satisfied. The fishing was good. Lovely hen trout in full spawning colours of silver or gold. Males, dark ebony and kyped with jaws like scimitars. The arctic charr iridescent in rainbow bibs of red and purple. One day carver knocked ten fine trout on the head and put them in a bag for me.

'Flesh firm and they smoke well, take them home to the bairns.' A peace offering though we weren't at war.

Our times in the shed were longer and longer as the weather worsened. The boy racers had found other amusements, lately gathering magic mushrooms from the sheltered birch hillsides across the road.

I was learning that Roderick wasn't daft – he was just quiet (like myself) and that carving for him was a therapy against mental agitation, for his mind was always far away from his carvings. He only carved adders.

While the boys were crossing the road he said: 'I make serpents right enough but what shapes a man for good or evil?'

'Rain's off, shite,' interrupted the boy racers and we went down to the loch. I rowed oars deep into the grey mist rising from the calm loch, craning my neck for rocks along the dark shoreline, woodcarver calling out 'more left oar, more right.' By the time we got to the end of Hazel Island, we saw the dark funnel of snow and rain whipping down from the Coul. The waves slapped hard against the trees on the shore. We had just lifted the bag net, heavy with heaving fish.

'Drop it man, drop it. To the island shore…' The boat almost swamped twice but we pulled hard onto the pebble shore of the island. We pulled the boat up onto a duvet of moss. I tied it to a large willow.

We saw the boys pulling their own boat safely ashore beneath the cemetery. We stumbled into the deep moss. The island floor was covered in orange and red mushrooms. The forest was thick with rowan, birch, hazel and alder. We were well-sheltered. Thunder rumbled, lightning struck the mountains in the distance. The rain lashed the trees above us. The old man managed to light the pipe and began carving.

I knew this might be the last time I could ask him, before our temporary work ended.

'That thing, the boy racers said that day, about killing all those men...'

Carver removed the pipe and put down the folded knife. He shifted his weight as if to walk away, as he did in the shed that day.

Thunder growled over the hills. Waves sprayed and hissed over the small trees. The sky above was grey but gloved with black fingers. He looked up at the trees.

'Before the war, I was a young man, just married. I worked as a trainee gardener on an Argyll estate. The new laird was a strange man and wanted to give the estate completely over to shooting. The garden was a nuisance to him and he wanted me to learn stalking. He used to bring foreign guests over for grouse and deer. Sometimes, he held balls in the big house and we were all kept away then. There were often guests on the hills shooting. One day I was on the hills and I saw this other man over by the cliffs in the mist. He was lost and panicking and would easily have gone over the edge. I shouted at him to stay put, then lead him down to my cottage for a bowl of soup and dram. My wife gave him some dry clothes and I walked him back to the big house...'

The storm was blowing over and the loch was calmer but an even darker storm was blowing in from the hills. We would have

to run for it and get to shore or risk a night on the island. We ran to the boat. The old man took the oars and brought the boat to shore with no wasted motion, in a perfectly straight line.

We were busy for the rest of the week. On the next to last day, the boys had crossed the road. Woodcarver stopped carving and straightened up, while looking to the cemetery.

'A lot of my folk are there,' he said.

'I was telling you… one day I was sitting at my fire and the next month I in North Africa. Later, I was wounded at Anzio and called a hero. When I came home I took up wood carving – a good hobby for a forestry man.'

He looked over to see the racers punching each other, throwing magic mushrooms up into the air.

He talked quickly.

'That estate was interned during the war. We didn't have newspapers and magazines, so there was a lot we didn't know until much later. Christine, my wife, said one day: 'That man, that man we fed the soup to, is that not him?' It was *him* no doubt. We were kept away for good reason during those balls and gatherings. That man wasn't Ribbentrop, who we knew visited the estate. That man was himself. The man I rescued from the cliff was *Herr Hitler*, on an Argyll hunting estate in the years before World War Two…'

The boy racers ran towards the shed. The woodcarver handed me a perfect snake.

The Sons of Macomish

It began the night Ivan Murmansk flopped out his dark sweating penis in the bar of the Haddock Arms Hotel and waved his fish-gutting knife above it, saying: 'I vill cut zis ovv so hellp me iv evver I vould betray you!'

The mackerel blade shimmered above his unzipped trousers… the tension eased… he put 'it' back in his underpants, then quietly put the knife away. Thus the Sons of Macomish were born. Ivan himself, mackerel gutter on the good ship *Rasputin* eight days out of Murmansk, missing his wife Pushka and daughter Anushka, together pressed tightly in photos in a hard leather wallet in his back pocket. Ivan, whose English sounds like a chainsaw badly over-lubricated, dripping oil:

'dozh, dozh, zhizhin, zhizhin, tsts, tsts, ushka, ushka, tootka, tootka…'

And Killibegs, kicked off an Irish trawler for general laziness, plays the mandolin so badly that people buy him drinks not to play at all… who quotes the Easter Proclamation of 1916 backwards, can recite all Christy Moore's songs and generally enlivens pub conversations with snatches of the philosophy of Sir Boyle Roche, the great 18th century Irish eccentric: His favourite quotes from Sir Boyle: 'the greatest of all possible misfortunes is usually followed by an *even greater one*' or, 'why should we do anything for posterity, for what has posterity ever done for us?' Killibegs, a slender dark oil slick…

Local Highland lad, Conger, who must have a surname

somewhere: Mackenzie, MacLeod, MacDonald: short and thick like a Conger, so called because years before, lobster fishing with his uncle, a giant conger eel flipped down the front of his gansy and almost into the nether regions of his oilskin trousers; he punched the huge eel in the head, knocking it far into the sea...

Myself: Cree Dan, born of a Lewis father and full-blooded Cree mother in a sawmill near Flin-Flon Manitoba; Gaelic in one ear, Cree in the other; one language wet and cold, slithering over the brain like an octopus; the other a dry prairie heat of a tongue, a warming, drying fierce prairie wind. My grandfather rode the boxcars with Woodie Guthrie once on the way to Medicine Hat. I usually keep my words to myself because English swims deeper in my brain and must be brought forcibly to the surface like a snapping pike; sometimes all three languages are like so many billiard balls in my head, clanging and clacking...

Yet we are all sons of Macomish, wherever we come from, wherever we go to.

Macomish, Gaelic, 'son of Thomas', MacThomais, Mahomish. A perfect description somehow. Conger's favourite expression: 'Nae doubt', I doubt. Doubting Thomas. The sceptic, lone voice, nay-sayer.

Mahomish: home-ish, looking for a home; ma home, my home, homeless: in Russia, Ireland, Alba, Assiniboia.

Macomish: *komische* (German) = strange, unusual, odd; a perfect description: with no doubt, doubtless.

Hence, 'The Sons of the Doubter.'

Ivan (as I was saying) put his penis gently back into his trousers and put his mackerel machete back into a fur-covered sheathe. 'The fur of a woolly mammoth,' said Ivan once. Who could doubt it?

All this in the stench and ming of the Haddock Arms where Conger once said a person could fall asleep and wake up in

Shanghai; or find himself in the hold of a Bulgarian Klondyker stripped to his y-fronts. A smoky purple haze above the heads, dark smoky wood from the holds of dead ships; beards and gansies looming in and out of the sickly sweet odour of lager, rum and whisky: all wafted by the smell of sulphurous farts, puke and urine. The occasional tourist pops a clean head in only to withdraw it quickly in spasms of coughing. Tables of dark burnished wood where once Ivan's swarthy penis lay...

Killibegs: 'We'll be just like the Fianna or Superman: truth, justice and the Macomish way; stealing from the rich to give to the poor... giving succour to widows, raising orphans, bringing hope to the flotsam and jetsam of post-Thatcher Britain.'

Conger measures his speech the way he turns a net for repair, turning it over slowly many times then pushing it along for the next mending, in speech slower than heron flight: 'Nae doubt. Absentee landlordism, white settlerism, agoraphobia, holiday homes, but where to start man, where to start?'

But we started. Killybegs and I work well together. He has cigarette papers and tobacco but my butane lighter always works. Killybegs says it is not becoming for the Sons of Macomish to smoke; I say as long as we share skins and tobacco it will be OK. We rowed on the light treacle waves of a loch, in the local Estate rowboat: the result of a letter Killybegs wrote on his peculiar letterhead:

From the Bureau of Interstellar Psychology
Doctor Dermot O'Hanrahan, Lord Killybegs
Killybegs Estate

Dear Mr. Glasgullet, (Estate Factor)
I and my native tribal colleague Dan Grizzly Bear of
Assiniboia, are involved in scientific work concerning

various salmonid species. We are trying to gather data on the habits of the great cannibal trout Ferox, which I believe is the key to future discussions on the disappearance of sea trout in Scottish waters. We seek permission to do a series of studies – during prime spawning times – to determine the frequency and diet of these deep-water predators. We would use modified fyke nets to trap the fish, weigh and tag them and release them for further study. Pregnant female trout would be stripped of eggs for a spawning programme. We would be grateful for your assistance.

Yours sincerely,
Lord Killybegs, Fellow of the Irish Institute of Salmonid Studies

We took turns rowing on a windless October day. There was a sprinkling of snow on the high hills. White birches having shed most of their bright orange leaves, stood white and crisp against the rusted bracken. Herons watched from shallow reed beds as I pulled the net floats toward the boat. The fyke net is really just a long bag which allows fish to enter but closes in on escape attempts. Fish in the net rustled and exploded with fury as the net was hauled to the surface; the fish went towards the end of the bag where they fought for space: all a sparkling collage of golden trout, silver sea trout and the brightest orange-red of spawning charr. Our scientific work began. The firmest, fattest trout went into the boat for further 'study'. Killybegs and I barbecued them slowly in an old clean oil drum, over a cold smoke of oak chip – the fish soaked in a marinade my mother learned from the Assiniboine. We then took our scientifically smoked trout to various old folks' homes and to old-age pensioners in the district. It was a rich and good food, melting in toothless mouths. The old folks were always very

grateful. We didn't overdo it. Many fish were released, especially the dark torpedo-shaped *ferox* – ugly snapping brutes.

'They are survivors, let them live,' said Killybegs, two cigarettes hanging from his mouth – the same Lord Killybegs of the Irish Institute of Salmonid Studies, Dept. of Interstellar Psychology.

Ivan Murmansk of the menacing mackerel blade and Conger weren't idle for the Doubting Brotherhood either, both men far less subtle in their approach than Killybegs and myself: advocates of direct Highland action. Ivan had a near fetish about tools for cutting, snipping, ripping, etc. (Too long with the mackerel we reckoned). He had an old Lada Riva toolbag (supplied with the car) stamped with Cyrillic letters which Ivan said meant 'cut the bastard open'. His kit contained bolt cutters and a lethal hacksaw. Conger behind the wheel of a blue N-reg Ford Escort, scouring the country roads for NO TRESPASS, KEEP OUT, PRIVATE ESTATE signs. Cut bolts, hack chains. Ivan had an impressive bag of padlocks and chains which he slowly restored and took back to Murmansk for whatever purpose. This night was a soft rain. The pale moon swam in its sheen.

The gate would not budge.

'Easy man, easy,' said Conger, his nose dripping down his ripped oilskins.

Ivan swears through his beard, in a disturbing rising crescendo:

'Zha, Zha, Zhizhin, *Shschit, Shschit…*' He rattles the chains which sets the dogs barking and lights shining from the nearby house; the chain works loose and the boys resort to the old Highland trick of lifting a locked gate off its hinges; then Ivan Murmansk stands in the rain like Atlas, spinning the wrecked gate over his head and far out into the burn, knocking a

PRIVATE FISHING ONLY sign into the burn with it. The gate points heavenward for an instant and sinks; the two run squelching over the slippery dying bracken. Ivan curses the padlock that got away.

Killybegs blew the foam from the top of his Murphy's.

'Well, bhoys, the International Brigade has done well so far. Food to the aged and infirm, metal for international alchemy…'

Tombstone Tormod, the local country-western singer bellowed out:

'It looks like they got a tiger by the tail…'

Only it comes out this way:

'*Het luiks lik they hgot a ticher by the ttell.*' Tombstone was in full gear and we had to wait for him to stop singing before we could hear Killybegs, who had set up another round.

'Surely, they don't have us tigers by the tail.'

'I doubt yer right,' said yer man, Conger.

The rain crashed against the sea-facing window while big Tombstone stepped up a gear. His bass player was pissed and missing notes but the crowd was focused on Tombstone and definitely not paying any attention to a massive bearded man, a dark lick of a man, a poetic Cree and a local man named after a fish.

'I doubt Rocky is next,' said Conger. We all drank to that.

'Rocky' was a near life-size statue who lived in a clump of bracken on a sea-cliff overlooking the village; the stone so faded, chewed and clarted that it looked more like a standing stone than a man who married into a wealthy Sussex family who had flirtations with Nazism before the war; in fact, Rocky's human version was once photographed with Goring and Streicher before being totally discredited after the war. Whence, he finally retired to another estate in England. The sculpture was placed lovingly on the exact spot where the Nazi admirer once gralloched his first stag on blood-soaked ground.

Local opinion towards Rocky was surprisingly divided; mainly because Rocky's grand-nephew still owned thousands of acres of land locally, including pubs (not the Haddock Arms, too down market) and shops. This lump of rain-riddled granite touched indirectly on many lives: stalkers, shepherds, house-keepers, estate workers who cooed about the statue and even decorated it on festive days. Rocky was in turn resented, tolerated, ignored and sentimentalised. And it stood, through wind and rain, hail and snow. Rocky bided, thrawn. Stags rubbed their rank sex on him. Stonechats shit on him. Dogs pissed on him. Yet Rocky stood. Rumours abounded about Rocky: protected by laser beams, electrical alarms. etc.

'Bollocks,' said Conger. 'Rumours put out by Rocky's hyphenated relatives.'

We didn't draw lots but we knew who would do it. Ivan was the strongest and was the only one who could do a real demoli-tion job on Rocky. I volunteered as more sure of the terrain than anyone else. I also had the best excuse of all: I was in the local angling club which fished the nearby lochs so my appearance up there was not all that unusual. Ivan and I would fish until dark then do the real business of the sons of Macomish: the destruc-tion of an idea; doing what others were afraid to do.

We had to get Ivan to promise a quiet and clean method. We nervously assured him that no oath would be necessary as we anticipated the sharp glistening blade of the mackerel knife. We were glad to simply take his word for it this time – no doubt!

We walked out in May. Gorse fiery on the hill, warm lizards and sloe worms crawled over the path; butterflies hovered over drinking bees. Two anglers, rods over their shoulders, one of them with a big fishing bag, big enough for spare reels, nets, and much more besides.

We each caught several trout in the heat of the day: fish still lean from the winter, brown gold against the soft grass. Night came in patches. Ivan stood against the horizon, sturdy under a few early stars. He folded his rod carefully, motioning me to the hillock where Rocky stood, gnarled and petrified. We saw the twinkling lights of the village and of ships at sea. There was a heat mist rising from the sea, distorting everything. I've told the story many times since. Ivan broke a strand of gorse and approached Rocky warily. He prodded the stone carefully for lasers or electric alarms. Ivan spread his bag on the grass, removing fishing reels, nets and one large sledge hammer neatly separated into three pieces! Ivan leaned one piece against his shin and carefully screwed all the pieces together. He repeated something softly in Russian, then spit into his hands. I can still hear the spit; a whispered hiss. The big Russian then began to chant softly at first, then louder and louder. It was definitely a Russian version of Leadbelly's 'take this hammer, carry it to the Captain' and when he came to the well-known shout *'Hut!'* he brought the hammer around and with a metallic clang, sparks leaping from the hammer head. Rocky's left arm leapt away into the night!

It wasn't that dark, being May, I could see the Russian's teeth flash in the darkness and more quickly this time, the sledge hammer connected with stone and the statue's right arm fell limply straight down into the deep grass at the statue's base.

Then, a cine camera could take over now. A man walks to the rear of the armless stone. Drops hammer to the ground, gurgles deep from the throat, spits into hands; huge hammer connects to pitted stone; nothing happens, huge man staggers to the ground, hammer spinning away. Man growls: in 'ZHAS, scschas and lizh, lizh, LIZH, LIZH,' repeats the blow. Metallic crack, hollow, stone head flies far out over the mist and a splash is heard far below. The head is gone.

From the depths of what is left of the stone man, a spaghetti jack-in-the-box of electrical cables begins to hiss and burn, spewing sparks in a bright pinwheel; then a high-pitched noise began, searing, painful. Lights came on illuminating the huge man with the hammer towering high above the stone. Burling and burling, the man-bear grunts and grunts, heaving the hammer far over a wall of mist. There was a very loud splash.

We sit in the Haddock Arms Hotel, doubting everything. Ivan is buying rounds. It will soon be winter. Locals are nodding and winking and saying only 'Aye, aye,' in that powerful totemic way that nevertheless says everything; everything because the drawn-and-quartered Rocky is still hollow: one massive lump of melted electrical stench from which dark crows drink. That alarm woke an entire village who saw only mist and sparks and a few lurking shadows.

Ivan, Killybegs, Conger and myself (whose Cree soul is cut cleanly in two by a dark ocean). Full of doubt, the original Thomas had to touch the bleeding wounds in Christ's side in order to remove his doubts. Right enough.

Someday, when the rain has stopped, the sons of Thomas will steal up the hill, through primroses the colour of a new moon, dip our hands into the hollows of that former stone-man and drink clear, pure water. We will put our hands into those wounds, but hope for a very different kind of resurrection.

Meanwhile, there is still much work to do.

Of that, there is no doubt.

about the author

Tom Bryan was born in Canada in 1950, of Scottish and Irish background. Long resident in Scotland, he is a widely published poet and fiction writer. He lived for many years in Stratheanaird, Wester Russ, which provided the inspiration for most of these stories. He now lives in Selkirk in the Scottish Borders.

The story *The Sons of Macomish* won first prize in the Two Rivers Press 1999 Short Fiction Competition